## Hello, Family Members,

Learning to read is one of the most important accomplishments of early childhood. **Hello Reader!** books are designed to help children become skilled readers who like to read. Beginning readers learn to read by remembering frequently used words like "the," "is," and "and"; by using phonics skills to decode new words; and by interpreting picture and text clues. These books provide both the stories children enjoy and the structure they need to read fluently and independently. Here are suggestions for helping your child *before*, *during*, and *after* reading:

### Before

- Look at the cover and pictures and have your child predict what the story is about.
- Read the story to your child.
- Encourage your child to chime in with familiar words and phrases.
- Echo read with your child by reading a line first and having your child read it after you do.

### During

- Have your child think about a word he or she does not recognize right away. Provide hints such as "Let's see if we know the sounds" and "Have we read other words like this one?"
- Encourage your child to use phonics skills to sound out new words.
- Provide the word for your child when more assistance is needed so that he or she does not struggle and the experience of reading with you is a positive one.
- Encourage your child to have fun by reading with a lot of expression . . . like an actor!

### After

- Have your child keep lists of interesting and favorite words.
- Encourage your child to read the books over and over again. Have him or her read to brothers, sisters, grandparents, and even teddy bears. Repeated readings develop confidence in young readers.
- Talk about the stories. Ask and answer questions. Share ideas about the funniest and most interesting characters and events in the stories.

I do hope that you and your child enjoy this book.

—Francie Alexander
  Reading Specialist,
  Scholastic's Learning Ventures

*To my girls:*
*Renata, Michelle, Amanda, and Michaela Anne*
*—E.T.*

*For Cinda Hoeven,*
*who taught Michael to read.*
*—S.B.*

Text copyright © 1999 by Edith Tarbescu.
Illustrations copyright © 1999 by Steve Björkman.
All rights reserved. Published by Scholastic Inc.
SCHOLASTIC, HELLO READER, CARTWHEEL BOOKS and associated logos are trademarks and/or registered trademarks of Scholastic Inc.

Library of Congress Cataloging-in-Publication Data
Tarbescu, Edith.
   Bring back my gerbil! / by Edith Tarbescu ; illustrated by Steve Björkman.
   p.   cm.— (Hello reader! Level 4)
   Summary: Best friends Caitlin and Tyler are surprised when she tries an experiment with his gerbil and apparently turns him into a dog.
   ISBN 0-439-09835-1
   [1. Gerbils Fiction. 2. Dogs Fiction.]   I. Björkman, Steve, ill.   II. Title.
III. Series.
   PZ7.T1653Br   1999
[E]—dc21                                                                99-15263
                                                                              CIP

10  9  8  7  6  5  4  3                                          0/0   01   02

Printed in the U.S.A.                                24
First printing, November 1999

# Bring Back My Gerbil!

by Edith Tarbescu
Illustrated by Steve Björkman

**Hello Reader! — Level 4**

SCHOLASTIC INC.    Cartwheel ·B·O·O·K·S·®
New York   Toronto   London   Auckland   Sydney
Mexico City   New Delhi   Hong Kong

# Chapter 1

Tyler laughs at my riddles and jokes.

That's why he's my best friend.

That's also why I let him call me Katie.

Everybody else has to call me Caitlin.

My second best friend is Jake.

He doesn't laugh at my jokes.

That's because Jake is Tyler's gerbil.

When people say, "How could Jake be a best friend?"

I tell them, "Gerbils have feelings, too."

One day, our teacher asked us to bring in

something for Sharing Time.

I raised my hand and asked if

I could bring in an animal.

"Sure," she said.

When I told Tyler I needed to borrow Jake,

he said, "What are you going to do with him?"

Before I knew what I was saying,

I blurted out, "We're going to clone him.

Then there will be lots of Jakes."

"Make a twin of him? No WAY," said Tyler.
"I like him just the way he is."

"I'm only kidding," I told him. "We wouldn't
know how to clone him anyway."
Tyler stared at me through his glasses.
Finally, he said, "Do you promise
to take care of him?"
"I promise," I said. "Let's go home and clean out
his cage. Tomorrow is a big day for Jake."

When we got off the school bus, two big kids
started teasing Tyler about his glasses.
"I wish I had a dog who would bark
at those kids," said Tyler.
"Maybe we can feed Jake something
that will turn him into a big dog," I said.
Tyler looked at me as if to say, *Could we?*
"Impossible," I answered.

# Chapter 2

But we tried. We tried everything.
Jake just ran around on his wheel and
ignored the food we offered him.

"Wait here," I told Tyler. "I'll be right back."
I ran next door to my house and
dashed into the kitchen.
I filled a small glass halfway with water.
Then I looked in the cabinet
and saw vanilla and almond flavorings.
I poured some in, along with
green food coloring;
the kind my mom uses
for baking cookies.

13

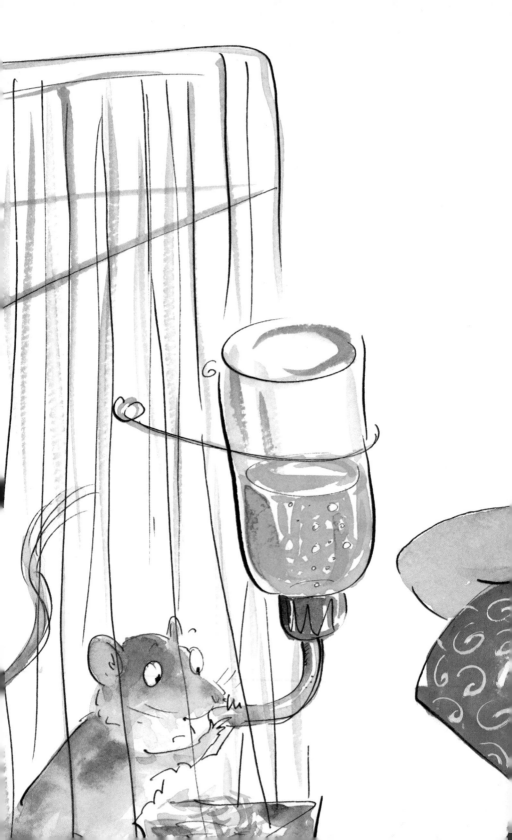

I shook it up and thought,
*What a magic brew this is.*
As soon as I got back to Tyler's house,
we poured it into Jake's bottle.
"Abracadabra," I said, over and over
as Jake started drinking.
"Are you trying to poison him?" shouted Tyler.
"Of course not," I answered.
"Forget it," said Tyler. "I like Jake
just the way he is."

I stuck the empty beaker in my pocket.

"It was your idea," I said.

Tyler turned around and faced me. "It was yours."

That was our first fight.

I kept saying, "Yours."

And he kept saying, "Yours."

Finally, we bumped into Jake's cage
and knocked it over.
Before we knew it, Jake ran out of the room.
"Oh, no," said Tyler. "Now look what you've done.
You know my mom's allergic to fur.
She'll kill me for letting him loose."

"No, she won't," I said. "When she starts sneezing, we'll know where he is."

"Sure!" said Tyler. "When she starts sneezing, she'll make me give Jake away."

"I'll help you look for him," I said.
I got down on my hands and knees and
started calling, "Here, Jake. Here, boy."
"He's not a dog," said Tyler. "He won't come
if you call him."
"If you had trained him,
he might have," I answered.
"You can't train a gerbil," said Tyler.

# Chapter 3

We crawled around until we bumped into something that was walking on four legs, and it was much bigger than a gerbil.

It was tan with white spots.
And it had black specks on its ears and
a short, stubby tail that stuck out
like a broom handle.
It looked like a dog!
Tyler said, "Could it be Jake?"
I didn't say anything.
I just stared at the dog.

"He looks just like Jake," cried Tyler.
"He's even the same color. And those
black marks on his ears are the same, too."

"Don't be silly," I told him.

"This must be a lost dog."

"Lost dog?" said Tyler. "In my hallway? Okay,
then tell me how he got in my house?"

I crept back a little. "Well…
maybe the front door is open. Let's go check."
We ran through the kitchen
and headed for the front door.
It was locked.

"I bet I'll never see Jake again," said Tyler.

I took off my headband.

I needed to think.

"We better get this dog in your room—with the door shut—before he starts barking and your mother hears him."

So we took Jake the Second into Tyler's room.
"We have to find some way to turn this
dog back into a gerbil," I said.
As soon as we closed the door, Tyler whispered,
"How can he be Jake the Second?
Jake the First is a gerbil.
This is a dog."

"I know," I said. "But just look at him.
He looks like Jake. You said so yourself."
Tyler's face was getting red. He said, "Well, then,
feed this dog what you fed the other Jake
and turn him back into a gerbil."

I looked around the room, not knowing what to do. "There isn't any left," I said, fumbling with the empty beaker inside my pocket. "I'll go call my dad and ask him what to do."

# Chapter 4

"Wait," shouted Tyler. "Don't go yet.
I always see signs about lost dogs and cats."
So, we got a big sheet of paper
from Tyler's closet and made up a poster.
"FOUND. Beautiful tan and white dog.
Owner, please call Caitlin."

We put my phone number on the sign.
Then we nailed the sign to a pole
in front of my house.
We went back to Tyler's house and
continued looking for Jake.

"What was it you fed him?" Tyler asked again.
"I told you. It was just plain water...
with a little coloring. It was supposed
to be a joke."

"Some joke," said Tyler.

I looked down at the floor and bit my lip.
"I think we ought to name this dog,"
I said, trying to change the subject.
I suggested Jake Boy.

Tyler said the name made him sad.
It reminded him of his gerbil.

We ended up naming the dog Frank.
Of course the dog didn't answer
to that name.
But we started teaching him.
We used a ball as a reward.
Frank was smart. He learned fast!
When it was time to go home,
I took Frank with me.

# Chapter 5

When I got home, my sister, Jessie,
was the first to see Frank. She fell in love with him.
She asked if she could trade me two stuffed
animals in exchange for Frank.
"You think I'm stupid?" I answered.
"Besides, he's not my dog."

Next, my mother bumped into Frank.

"And who is *this*?" she asked.

"He's Frank," I told her. "He belongs to Tyler."

My mother looked confused. "I thought
Tyler's mother was allergic to fur.
Isn't that why he got a gerbil,
so it could stay in Tyler's room?"

"Yup," I answered.

I didn't even *try* to explain what happened.
Instead, I waited until my dad got home.
I thought, *He works in a lab. He'll understand.*
"You see," I told everyone during dinner,
"Tyler and I did this experiment and Jake,
the gerbil, turned into a dog..."

Jessie almost choked on her milk.

My mom dribbled soup down her chin.

Only my dad didn't move.

"What did you feed him?" he asked.

"Water…" I mumbled.

I was about to tell him about adding
vanilla, almond, and green food coloring
when the phone rang.

My father listened for a while,
then said, "Hold on, please."
The woman on the phone was looking for a
lost dog who answers to the name of "Sugar."
I called Frank "Sugar," but he didn't turn around.
Dad invited the woman to come over
and see the dog for herself.

The phone rang two more times,
and the same thing happened.
In a little while, three strangers
stood in our living room.
They all came to see Frank,
or whatever his real name was.

# Chapter 6

The three strangers left,
then a tall blonde girl arrived.
She looked at the dog and yelled, "Shadow!"
Frank ran over to her.
"Shadow, I missed you so much."
The girl bent down and began
hugging and kissing Frank.

She turned to me and smiled.

"Thanks for taking such good care of him.

If your folks will drive you to my house,

you can play with Shadow anytime."

"You mean it?" I asked.

"Any friend of Shadow's is a friend of mine."

She gave me her phone number.

Then she left with Shadow.

I ran over to Tyler's house

to tell him the news.

When I reached Tyler's bedroom,
there, on top of his bed,
was a little ball of fur. It was Jake!
"Where did you find him?" I asked.
"He was curled up in the back of my closet.
Where's Frank?" asked Tyler.

I told him the story of Shadow and his owner.

That's when Tyler said he had

something to tell me, too.

"You know when we checked

the front door? Well, you went back

to my room after that.

But I checked the back door, and it was open."

"Why didn't you tell me?" I shouted.

"I wanted to play a trick on you," said Tyler.

"That was mean," I said. "I never did that to you."

"You did, too," he answered.

"You wanted me to think

you turned Jake into a dog."

"That was different," I answered.

Tyler sat still for a moment. Then he said, "You can take Jake to school any time you want. Just don't try to clone him."

"I don't know how to clone animals.
I'm only in third grade, like you."

The next day was my turn for Sharing Time.
I held up the cage with Jake inside and said,
"Guess what? Yesterday this gerbil
was a dog!"